AGONY OF THE WORLD

A POST-APOCALYPTIC STORY

BOYD CRAVEN III

Agony Of The World, The World Burns Book 9
By Boyd Craven
Many thanks to friends and family for keeping me writing!

To be notified of new releases, please sign up for my mailing list at:
http://eepurl.com/bghQb1

1

JOHN NORTON, TEXAS

"Caitlin, are they still following us?" John asked into the earwig of one of the radios they had scavenged and repurposed.

"Yeah, half a mile back. Those boys are in a hurry to catch up with us," her voice crackled in reply.

"Ready for company," Tex's voice came through clear.

It should have, John was at the north end of what looked like a box canyon. They had been staging hit and run attacks against the New Caliphate for weeks now. They'd suffered only slight injuries, but John's group of volunteers had swelled faster than he could train them. So instead, he started sending people north towards Kentucky, where Sandra and Blake resided. He led the central portion of the sappers that had been harrying the invaders, chipping away at them.

When they first engaged them at Laughlin Air Force Base, John and everyone else involved had significantly underestimated their foe. Instead of goat herders handed an AK and a zeal for Muhammad, they were competent fighters and had repositioned the mortar teams under the group's nose. Even with the warning, Laughlin was overrun.

"Get out of there Tex, fall back to where Caitlin is going to come through."

"Got it," Tex replied in his lazy drawl.

A dust cloud kicked up in the distance, and John watched dispassionately as the old 4x4 Blazer raced through the dry land of West Texas. Caitlin and a small team had staged a mortar attack of their own, hitting in the flanks of the advancing troops. A detachment had split off to give chase. Until now, they had only chipped away at their numbers but, with the materials they had mixed and stashed, they were hoping to cut them down drastically.

"Come on girl," John mumbled to himself, his thumb on the button of the detonator, praying she didn't get a flat or wipe out from hitting one of the many outcroppings of sandstone that seemed to rise up at the last instant.

He hadn't realized he was holding his breath until she was through with her truck, and then John made his way over to the dirt bike he'd stashed. Getting on it, he fired it up and waited. More than a dozen trucks, and a troop carrier the Caliphate had stolen from somewhere, came barreling into the pass, hoping to bottle up Caitlin and her small team.

"Fire in the hole," John murmured, depressing the button.

The explosion seemed to suck all the oxygen out of the crisp fall air and, when the shockwave and sound hit, it looked as if a train had come off the tracks and hit the side of the mountain. The ground rumbled and the noise deafened John, but he stood there watching as the entrance to the pass collapsed, making it impossible to back out. He kick-started the dirt bike and raced along a trail almost at the top of the canyon wall, and saw that the column of Caliphate had stalled. Whether from confusion, shock, or the dawning realization that they were about to meet Jesus and not Allah, it didn't matter. Tex held the last detonator and all John had to do was drive past his location. A stream that had cut its way into the side of the hills gave the small canyon the look of a box canyon. It wasn't.

Rocks exploded in front of the bike and he swerved, knowing somebody had sighted him. He couldn't hear their motors running, but he gave a half a look back to make sure they were coming. They had started rolling, and he smiled grimly. Nobody in the team had wanted him to do this part, but he knew the greatest aspect of any trap was to have the right kind of bait. Caitlin was the first bit, and John was the second. Pouring on speed, he wound out the two-stroke bike for all it was worth, holding on to keep from flying over the handlebars as he raced down the side of the wall, towards the ground level.

"Now!" he heard Caitlin scream as the bike shot past Tex.

He'd made it, and the adrenaline was making everything seem as if it was working in slow motion. He hit the back brake and put a foot down, sliding the rear wheel 180 degrees, and motored back to where Caitlin had parked as the land he'd just left erupted. The charges had been dug in and, when they went off, a mountain of rock just slumped towards the middle of the gap. Where there had been probably sixty men chasing after them in vehicles, now only a pile of rubble remained. They closed their mouths and pulled up bandanas as the dust billowed out.

"Mop up?" Tex asked.

"Yeah, and scavenge anything we can. That troop carrier will be a bonus if it isn't wrecked."

"I'm pretty sure everything's wrecked sugar," Caitlin said, her accent thick when she was worked up.

"I know, but even ammo at this point would be helpful. It isn't like the government is doing our resupply. Have somebody get on top of the ridge and watch to see if they send more people to check on these guys. We need to be ready to move out fast if that's the case."

"On it boss," Tex said.

For the first time since Laughlin had been lost, Tex broke into a grin. This was his home state, and seeing how the invaders had been treating the Americans and the land, had been heartbreaking for him. Now they had some real payback. They had cut down more than those that had died in the canyon this day, but it was by small numbers. Doing this had been calculated to remove material support, as in trucks and weapons, as much as anything else.

"LOOKS LIKE WE'VE GOT MORE 7.62X39 THAN WE CAN HAUL home, there's three AK47s left intact, and we can probably Frankenstein a couple dozen more from the stuff we scavenged."

"What about RPGs?" John asked.

"About that," Caitlin said, pulling at the ends of her hair, "Launchers are no good, but we were able to scavenge two crates of grenades for them."

"Vehicles?" John asked.

"None worth spending time on," Tex answered. "But I know you want that troop carrier. I've got a few guys digging out the front end, to see if we can get it up and over the rest of the rubble. By the way, the guy we pulled out of the center truck died. Nobody to interrogate."

John cursed; he'd been hoping for one to talk to. Instead, they'd done their jobs all too well.

"I just wish the president wasn't working against us here," John groused for the hundredth time.

"Why's he got you locked in his sights?" Stu asked, having joined up with them after Laughlin.

"You weren't there for the start of things," Tex said. "John here shook up the South before people knew it needed shaking up."

"What do you mean?" Stu asked.

"Broke some folks out of FEMA camps that were being run by an Eastern European gangster named Lukashenko," John told him. "Apparently he's related to somebody with the same name, or has some serious pull with our president. Anyway, we tore the walls down at his camp, and he slipped away. I thought he was still in the wind but my son's friend, Michael, and King saw him murdered by some of his own men. They blame me for that."

"Wait, were these the camps where they were...? Making the women and ladies...?"

"Yeah," John said hurriedly, "But sometimes there's only two things the people upstairs care about: money and power. This Lukashenko was a conduit to one or the other to our government, and they blame me for throwing a monkey wrench into the works. Don't worry, though; they want me, they just won't supply the folks with me unless I turn myself in."

"We're doing just fine, don't ya think?" Caitlin asked.

Stu always got tongue tied around her, and she knew it. She used that to her advantage whenever the younger soldier started asking a ton of questions when he should be hustling or paying attention to anything else.

"We got a live one," Tex yelled as a dirty, dusty and

bloody man was pulled from underneath the troop carrier. "Somehow got between the front tires, under it."

The gash across his forehead was almost blinding him with blood, and he kept wiping at it with the one arm that wasn't broken, smearing red across his tan robes.

"We good here? Anybody see anything coming?" John asked.

"No, I just heard from the watchers, and we're clear. The main body kept right on rolling," Stu said after a moment, dragging his eyes away from the former Miss America model.

"Good, get him over to medical," John told Tex, smiling. "Patch him up, and we'll talk."

"Good deal, and then?"

"We're going to get ahead of them. They are going after Air Force installations. I'm worried they are trying to gain control of, or disable our nukes."

"Shoot," Caitlin said. "We have to stop that."

"Yeah, put a call into Sandra on scramble. Our fearless leader may not resupply us or give us good intel, but Sandra will via Michael and King."

2

DUNCAN & SANDRA, THE HOMESTEAD KENTUCKY

"Grandpa?" Chris yelled.

"Hey buddy," Duncan said, catching the boy as he almost ran into him, and Supermanning him in the air.

"Put me down," the little boy giggled. "Mom says she needs you in the barn. She's got some new recruits and wants you to take over."

"Is her stomach hurting again?" Duncan asked, putting him down.

"No, she says the body snatcher is hungry, and her tummy is growling at the class. The guys keep cracking up, and she says if she doesn't get something to eat, she's going to crack them up if they keep cracking... Grandpa, what's cracking up mean?"

Duncan smiled and mussed the boy's hair as they walked. He'd been sitting on the porch, having had his blood pressure taken by one of the medics that had come to be stationed there at the Homestead. It was almost under control, and Duncan had been dropping weight faster than he'd thought possible. No longer did he have chest pains, but years of abusing his body and heart had made him worry that overworking himself would provoke a heart attack.

"Where's your dad? He around?"

"He's down at the Smith's farm," Chris said, turning to wave at Melissa who had walked out with Bobby. She waved back and blew him a kiss. Chris acted like he caught it and then proceeded to pretend to eat it very loudly. "Mwah mwah mwah."

"Hey, don't do that. Someday you'll want girls to give you kisses."

"Like you and Grandma?"

"Something like that. Now, don't you have schoolwork you should be doing?"

"It's Saturday," Chris giggled, "there's no school on Saturdays unless you're a soldier and then the school is every day."

"Well, I guess that's okay."

"Chris, come get lunch," Lisa's voice drifted out from behind them.

"Okay!" he called back.

Before he could shoot off, Duncan stopped him. "Tell her that your mom is going to be hungry too. Tell her I said to make her a double triple-decker."

"What's that?" Chris asked, all serious now.

"A heart attack sandwich," Duncan told him, smiling.

"That sounds gross. Hey, after you're done, can we play some Battleship or Uno?"

"Sure thing, kiddo." Duncan mussed the boy's hair again, and he took off like a shot.

"...And it's reassembled like this." Sandra was finishing as Duncan walked in.

"Oh, Daddy!" she said excitedly and put down the receiver of an AR-15 and gave him a hug.

Her stomach was pronounced on the normally whip-cord thin woman. The bottom of her shirt barely covered her baby bump, making it hard for her to lean over and give her father a hug. If he hadn't been losing weight, they never would have made it. As it was, their embrace was as warm as always. Duncan saw the glow of happiness in his daughter and thanked the Lord for her, for Blake and for their new direction in life.

Somebody coughed behind her, and someone else snickered. The rest were almost ready to crack up when Bobby and Melissa walked in. Melissa was part of Sandra's squad, and everyone quieted down. They knew her squad consisted of all very capable and determined women, but none of the men in the room had seen Sandra do more than rub her aching back, her stomach or teach them about guns, tactics, and theory. She was an unknown to them, other than a legend.

"Something funny?" Bobby asked in an offhand manner to the forty men and a few women mixed in the open doorway of the barn where the class was taking place.

"Well, it's just that... she's all baby, and she had to get on her tip toes and..."

Sandra shot her dad a mischievous look, and Duncan shook his head.

"How many of you have done your hand-to-hand training with me?" Bobby asked.

Half the hands in the room shot up, including some of the women.

"How about me?" Melissa asked.

Almost all hands shot up, making her smile and jab him in the ribs.

"Well, before Sandra got too far along in her pregnancy, she taught me everything I know," Bobby said. "Melissa as well."

More than a few jaws fell open. Bobby was slowly putting on muscle and gone was the young, lanky kid who had first wandered onto the Homestead, running from a gang of raiders and rapists. Now stood a young man who was sure of himself, of his abilities, and who had a direction in life. He'd taken on a lot since Blake had left to try to show the other camps why his were outperforming everyone else's. One of the things that Bobby and Melissa had taken on, other than their regular duties, was teaching hand-to-hand basics. They were known for being an almost unbeatable team and had often had half the class come at them at once.

"Don't look at him like that, I heard the first time Bobby met Sandra, he hit on her," Melissa said, and even more jaws dropped as they swiveled to look at her fiancé, and Bobby was smiling and nodding in agreement.

"Well, let's just say I got my butt handed to me," Bobby said.

A hand raised toward the back, and Sandra stood on her toes and pointed to the woman. "Jessica, is it? You have a question?"

The crowd of people parted, leaving a young woman standing in a small empty pocket. She started talking, but Sandra couldn't hear her, so she motioned with her hands for Jessica to come toward the front.

"Ma'am, I'm not doubting what they're a sayin'," jessica's Cajun accent came through clear, "but you'se so tiny. I'd like to learn how to not be... I don't ever want a man to be able to..."

"If I can do it," Sandra said, "so can you. If you, or anyone else, wants to learn more advanced techniques than the basics we're teaching at this site, I can set aside some time to work with folks on a one-on-one basis."

"Not until you have that baby, ma'am," Bobby cut in, "but I'd be more than happy to work under your direction so you don't pop early."

"Yeah, I'm good with that too," Melissa said, putting her arm in Bobby's.

"So..." Duncan said after clearing his throat loudly, "... what are we teaching this group today?"

"Field stripping different weapons. We are on the AR-15 currently, showing them the differences in the bolt carrier and auto sear compared to what we have here in the civilian model. Next up are the AKs and then some Israeli gear we recovered. The basics."

Duncan rubbed his hands together in anticipation. He loved his guns and, as the former armorer for the Homestead, before it was turned into a small training ground, he was happy to get his hands back in the gun oil again.

"That sounds great! Hey, I asked Lisa to fix you something, it should be ready. When's lunch for this group?"

"We just ate, sir, we're her third group in a row," Jessica answered before anyone else could talk.

In response to that, Sandra's stomach let out an audible grumble, and she held her hands over her belly and looked at her father and then at the door. He pointed with his thumb, and she gave him a thousand-watt smile and hurried off.

"Her feet are killing her too," Melissa whispered as she and Bobby left as well.

Duncan took a deep breath and looked around the room. Lots of eager faces awaited him. What they were learning here at the Homestead wasn't the same as they would have gotten in boot camp. Everyone alive this long after the EMP attack was already a survivor of one sort or another. Instead, the training they were giving was meant to be a starting point, as the volunteers were assigned where they were needed. They would assist the growing population of military personnel that was either returning home from overseas, or coming back from helping their own families with the massive fighting that was breaking out all across the country.

In Texas, where the land-based war had started, there were already three large militia groups that were being reinforced with volunteers to help stop, or at least slow, the advancement of the New Caliphate. Still, looking at the mixed group of recruits, Duncan saw something in these young men and women that had been gone from the countryside for a while now. Hope. Hope, and a determination to hold onto the country they were born in.

"All right, looks like she's got the action back together. The rest goes back the same as..."

"Duncan?" Lisa's voice came over the handheld radio loud.

"Yes, dear," Duncan said smiling and watching grins light the faces of more than a few folks in the class area.

"What exactly goes on a double triple heart attack sandwich?"

The class cracked up, and Duncan shook his head, hiding a wry smile.

3

BLAKE, SMITH'S FARM, KENTUCKY

Blake had helped many a farmer fix things, but the harvest wasn't something he'd done by himself before. But he'd had plenty of volunteers and was now putting them to use. Silverman's mechanics had gotten every older tractor in the area working, and fuel supplies were being consolidated. All Blake had to do now was try to get an idea of the yield they were harvesting out of the corn and soybean fields and report back.

Much of the country was still crippled, but the older diesel locomotives were being located and were replacing the diesel/electric pushers that had taken over the industry. The parts for the old engines were easier to source than the hybrids, and if what Blake was experiencing here worked out, then much of the rest of the country might have a fighting chance of surviving the coming winter, not that there were many people left. He'd seen the figures from the government. 92% mortality already. And, with winter coming on, 8% of approximately 360 million people left less than thirty million people in the country. The United States couldn't afford to lose any more to starvation or the cold.

If enough people survived the starving times, disease, and the cold of winter, there might be enough people left to actually do something about the New Caliphate. Still, the country had been planted with crops and, with enough people in the know and with a way to transport things, they had a real chance of knocking starvation off the list of worries.

"Hey, Blake," Sgt. Silverman said. "Big man's on the horn."

"Which one?" Blake asked, wary.

"Not the *big* big man, the governor."

Blake sighed in relief. He had spoken with the president exactly twice now, and both times had left him feeling like a mouse that had fallen into the shadow of a hawk. He'd been a part of dismantling the local Kentucky government and, even if Boss Hogg being arrested for his misdeeds hadn't been enough, Blake had found out he was a friend of the president. Watching his wife kick Hogg's sweaty gluteus maximus up to his triple chin had been pretty amusing, but in the end, he worried every time he talked to the president over the radio.

"Blake here," Blake said into his earwig after tuning into the right frequency.

"Blake, you ready for some more travel?"

Blake groaned but kept that off key.

"No, I've been gone from my place for too long. After I finish the figures here at the Smith's farm I told you about, I'm going to send in my report. Sgt. Silverman has somebody who can make it look official even."

"Listen, they really want you to head to Massachusetts."

"Can't do that. Besides, I'm stepping down as director in a couple of weeks. Sandra's getting big, and I need to tend to my own doings at the Homestead."

"I could compel you not to step down," the governor said softly.

"Excuse me?" Blake asked, standing bolt upright.

Silverman had his ears in because he shot Blake a look that spoke of disgust and incredulity.

"This is how important your work with these camps is. They need you. The president needs you, the country needs you."

"It isn't up for debate. I've basically served my sentence already. I'm stepping down in a couple of weeks, and I'm spending this weekend with my family."

"Blake, like I said— "

"Go ask the former governor what happened last time he tried to compel us to do anything," Blake shot back, his blood boiling.

The line went silent, and Silverman looked at the quiet man in open shock. What they'd done at the Homestead was self-defense. Even the shelling of the governor could be seen as such, but to outright threaten the same thing again made Silverman cringe. Still, he would follow along with whatever Blake, Sandra, and Duncan cooked up. He owed them his life, time and time again, and the same went for his men.

"Blake, I didn't mean it to sound like that. They just really need you," the governor said after a long minute.

"I appreciate you telling me that, Governor, and I really meant what I said to you. This is why the FEMA programs across the country were doomed to fail and ignite a revolution. You were 'compelling' people to do what you wanted them to do. People will naturally want to come together and work for a common cause, especially if they and their families are fed and clothed. *Forcing* them to anything will only make them dig their heels in and lash out. Don't forget that.

What you just said has *me* digging my heels in. I just want to get back to a quieter life."

The governor cursed softly over the air, but not directed at Blake. His words spoke of being in an impossible situation with no visible options. When his tirade was done, he spoke to Blake directly again.

"I get that, and I'm sorry. Will you at least be available for consulting, talking over the radio like this?"

"That I don't mind. In fact, I plan on doing more Rebel Radio broadcasts," Blake said, not believing for one second they would just let him walk away.

"Good, that's good. Well, I uh... Listen, if I get a chopper out there Monday, could you make a trip to Mass so I can get the pres off my butt?"

"If you put it in writing that you're letting me walk when my sentence is up."

"Deal," the governor said, "Just be thankful they aren't asking you to go west."

"You mean because of the New Caliphate?"

"Yeah, they're attacking our Air Force installations. Texas through Nebraska and Colorado, so far."

"Nebraska? What's there?" Blake asked, looking and the fields of corn around him and imagining Nebraska to be much of the same.

"Strategic assets, apparently. I don't need to know, according to the higher ups. I just hope your wife's efforts with the Joint Chief's plans come to fruition. Otherwise, bacon is going to be banned in America."

"Now that would be a shame. Listen, I really am sorry for putting you on the spot like I did, but I don't want to ever be put in that situation again. I don't know why you thought—"

"Blake, truly. I'm sorry. I'm just frustrated, and right now, you're the closest thing we've got to a celebrity. You could do a lot of really really good things for the country if you stayed with FEMA."

"I think I can do great things at home too. Being a husband, father, and teacher. But... listen to Rebel Radio, later on tonight. I think maybe you're going to like our topic for the evening."

"Oh yeah, what's that?" His voice was mildly amused.

"Working with the government. Blake out," he said, and turned off his radio.

Silverman listened for a few more moments and then looked up at Blake, a smile running across his face. "You liked to have scared the daylights out of me, threatening the governor over open channels like that."

"Why's that?" Blake asked him mildly.

"I mean if word gets out..."

"I don't know if I heard it in a movie or if it's Jefferson or what," Blake said, "but it goes something like this: 'when the people fear their government, there's tyranny, and when the government fears their people, there's freedom.' Sometimes, it doesn't hurt to remind them of that fact. Otherwise, they seem to get too big for their britches."

"You're crazy," Silverman said.

"Pretty much. Hey, if I get these figures to you in the next twenty, can one of your men give me a lift back to the Homestead?"

"Sure thing."

4

MICHAEL & KING, NEBRASKA

"Something else is going on," Michael said to King, looking through a spotting scope.

King was lying flat on his stomach, a .338 Lapua looking like a toy gun in his meaty arms. He was watching a convoy that had approached the edge of a DHS outpost a few miles from a FEMA camp.

"Wind?" he asked.

"Five miles an hour, coming west to east. My spotter says a thousand meters," Michael whispered.

King made one adjustment on his scope, the click of the knob louder than the wind rustling the surrounding corn that had been planted all around the machine shop they were now lying on the roof of.

"Can you make out what they are saying?" Michael asked.

"Don't read lips," King replied softly.

He took in the slack in the trigger slowly, gently. When the rifle went off, it surprised him slightly, as it should. He'd been slowing his breathing to time the shot between his heartbeats, a low point in the wind and hopefully when

Murphy was fast, fast asleep. The bullet hit high and to the right of the target. Instead of the tip of the nose, it entered the left eye of the New Caliphate's spokesperson. Michael and King saw pink mist and people hitting the deck.

"Hit," Michael said, as if King hadn't been watching already.

King grunted and sent more lead down the line. This was another hit, and the third was a bit low, but it hit the terrorist invader under the arm, in the top of the rib and armpit area. Return fire was starting, though none of it was even remotely close.

"Let's go," he said, and slid the rifle down to his side.

"Right behind you, big guy."

Sliding down the tin roof was easy, though it cost them in the form of super-heated skin that made them feel like they were being cooked. Motors fired up in the distance, audible over the gunfire that was starting to ping off the buildings near the small three corner intersection. There wasn't much out here, but the fact that the DHS and Jihadis were now firing on their position was both a comfort and distressing. It sucked because it somehow looked as if they were working together. It had been the third instance where they had witnessed something like this, but they'd never been fired upon by Americans before.

Hitting the bottom molding, King rolled onto his back and grabbed the .338 in big hands and let his feet dangle over the edge before dropping. He fell four feet before he hit the compressor room roof. It was a shed-like structure that made getting onto the main roof a cinch, especially as they still had the APC they had liberated after Texas.

"Here they come," Michael said, though both of them could hear the roaring of the engines.

"I got the wheel, you work as a gunner," King yelled as

his next hop landed him on the top of the APC and he dropped in through the hatch.

Michael had seen it a dozen or more times, and every time he expected the big man to get stuck, but it didn't happen. As far as King's orders went, they made sense to Michael. King was getting better at driving the APC, but Michael had taken to the entire machine as he was born in one. It didn't matter that the instructions were in Cyrillic, he'd proven that he could operate it efficiently. He also knew the difference between anti-personnel rounds and HE rounds now, a distinction that made everyone around his first use of the turrets sweat the sweat of the nervous, or the ones who knew they were very close to death.

"Two seconds," Michael said, folding the small adjustable tripod he'd been using with the spotting scope.

It wasn't one of the new digital models, but something right out of the Vietnam era, if he had to guess. Actually, Michael thought it was a lot newer, but it worked, and that was what counted. Hopefully.

"Hustle, boy," King said, smiling in the darkened interior.

"I'm ready," he said, closing the hatch and checking the load he had in the breach. "Reloading with HE round."

"Looks like one DHS APC inbound. No turrets. Light armor. Give it one."

King had gone back to short choppy sentences, but Michael knew the drill King was talking about. They had war-gamed this exact scenario. First would be high explosive, and if it still kept coming, they would send an armor piercing round next. The armor piercing round would be devastating to a small vehicle like the APCs they were in.

"Firing," Michael said as soon as he got a sight picture and hit the red button he'd learned meant it let it fly.

The gun fired overhead, and Michael was already working to open the breach, and reload in an armor piercing round. King fired up the twin diesels to give the turret more power and a faster response time because he could see the first round hit just in front of the APC, kicking up a big cloud of dust.

"Keep an eye on your windage. You missed."

"I one!" Michael yelled and hit the button again.

The big gun roared, and the round hit dead square on the American-made APC. Fire shot out from the seams, and it came to a dead stop. Still, the rag tag bunch of trucks and converted technicals raced down the highway towards them. Michael resisted the urge to duck, cringe or hide as the rounds from their light machine guns opened up, turning the inside of their APC into what Michael imagined a tuning fork would sound like if it were turned inside out.

"You won nothing, keep firing," King said, gunning the diesels and pointing the big slow Russian APC towards the lead vehicle. "It's a joke, from a battleship. Blake told it a month or so back. He and his kid were playing it, and he mentioned it on Rebel Radio."

Blake had, in Michael's mind, become something of a legend. He saw a lot of himself in the solitary man. Somebody who could survive on his wits alone and had. The one difference was the homesteader wasn't as much of a gun dog as Michael was turning out to be; he had had learned enough skills not to be a liability, whereas Michael wanted to become a weapon. One which he'd use against the people who had taken his father away and killed off much of the country. Lukashenko was directly responsible, but it was the Jihadis and North Koreans who made the situation possible.

"Firing," Michael said, using an AP round against the civilian vehicles.

"Grab something," King said, and the APC almost went on three wheels as he banked hard.

The heavy vehicle was designed with six tires, none of which were necessary if it were to cross water, but very necessary to race down the pitted asphalt. As it was, King put it in neutral and let the vehicle start coasting to a stop as he dropped a gun port, stuck the barrel of the .338 out and began firing. The result of both of them pouring the fire on was like adding gasoline to a fire made from pine trees. The Jihadis and DHS marked vehicles turned and tried to flee. For five minutes, Michael kept firing as long as he had a sight picture, knowing how far he could shoot with the turret.

"I think you got 'em," King said.

"I hope they won't be back." Michael watched their retreat as the two groups split up and headed in different directions.

"Hit the APC with HE," King told him.

Michael took a deep breath, reloaded and sighted in. At this distance, it was now an easy shot, and when the shock-wave hit and lifted the APC up and then down, they both felt the explosion and the impact, despite the vibrations of their own twin diesels.

"Why?" Michael asked after a moment.

"Perceived power. Remember your first day at Talladega?"

Boy, did he ever. How King had introduced himself, his advice on making a mark and never letting somebody perceive you as weak, unless you wanted to be a victim. He'd learned about power, dominance, and a ton of other things that were left unsaid but obvious, nonetheless.

"I do, thanks for the reminder."

"At least you didn't have to sleep with one hand over your— "

"Thanks for that mental image, buddy," Michael interrupted with a laugh that neither of them heard well. Their ears were ringing from both the inbound gunfire and the big gun as it had rained hell on earth down on the incoming vehicles. Still, they were both smiling. They had lived through the attack and spread the spearhead of the New Caliphate to the four corners of the map. More concerning, though, was the fact that they seemed to be meeting up with the DHS. Why?

"We need more intel. Call in what we saw. I'll be driving up to see if anybody needs triple A."

"Har har har," Michael said as he came forward to look out the viewports King had down.

"Anything moving?" Michael asked after a few moments of cruising the blacktop.

"Nope," King said, pulling to the side of the APC that had been shot up by them.

Michael went up through the hatch and wasn't surprised to hear the diesels shudder to a stop. King joined him, and they stood next to it, the machine giving off tremendous heat.

"Nobody survived that," Michael said pointing.

"Nope."

Walking around it, they could see the devastation their rounds had caused. Michael shielded his eyes and looked further into the distance at the other vehicles they'd disabled. Four mismatched trucks and a technical had come to a halt. The interiors were painted with safety glass and red. Not a pretty sight. Michael pulled his handset after looking at things and headed back into the APC. King stayed outside, walking closer to the DHS vehicle as it cooled. He wrote down the numbers on the side in a dog-eared notebook he'd taken to keeping in his tactical vest, and his scribbles were recorded by a half chewed pencil.

Looking to the distance himself, he made sure he had the old 1911 he favored. He did, plus four spare mags. He considered getting his M4 out, but decided against it and walked along the shoulder of the road. If anybody got cute, he knew Michael would pull the hatch and meet him for an exfil, but it wasn't a big worry. He could always ghost into the corn and lay low. What he knew the kid had seen, but hadn't commented on, were the human remains that had been partially sucked out the hole of the armored APC as the round exited the other end. The other vehicles he was walking toward had been hit with high explosives and anti-personnel rounds, basically a huge shotgun shell. It would be worse than what they'd seen here.

The gravel of the shoulder crunched under his feet. He felt Michael's eyes on his back and smiled. The kid had really grown into his role. Sandra had been his best student ever, even surpassing him in both skill and ability, but if given another year, Michael might be on par with even her. King felt weary, his life one war after another. Still, this was one worth fighting, one worth dying for if that was needed. If the Grim Reaper finally came to calling, he wouldn't begrudge him one bit.

His handset crackled, and King made sure the earwig was in. The gear was a mixed bag of captured gear, and they got a resupply drop once in a blue moon. Not much, usually ammunition and MREs. King mused that if they had even more ammunition they'd do more hunting instead of intel gathering, which was their primary mission anyway.

"What you see, big guy?" Michael's voice came in loud and clear.

"I see dead people," King replied in a mock whisper.

There was a shocked silence and then a feminine laugh broke the airwaves. King smiled so big, the whites of his teeth shone out brightly, even though nobody was there to see.

"Did you just make a joke?" Michael's mother's voice came in loud and clear.

"He does that sometimes," Sandra said from further away, "Usually it comes across as he's going to eat all the little children, so run… run away…"

"Monty Python? You're funny," King said back. "Yeah, I'm good. So far no survivors. Goons were meeting with DHS. DHS fired on us, so we took them out. Need you to pass this up the chain."

"Got some identification marks you can share?" Sandra asked, all business-like now.

He read them off to her.

"This isn't the first time we've seen something like this," Michael said after a pause.

"It isn't the first time I've heard of it either," Michael's mom agreed, from her outpost near St. Louis.

"How you two sitting for supplies?" Sandra asked.

"Got some MREs, half a case of toilet paper, and corn as far as we can see," Michael said.

King peered into the two burning wrecks of trucks that he walked up on. No survivors, perhaps some gear to scavenge if the fire from the HE round didn't damage everything. He walked to the next one, a white Ford that had come to rest on its side. Nobody inside was moving either. He leaned in the side window and felt the neck of a dark skinned man who was buckled in. No pulse. No way the driver was alive. He started towards a Nova, one of the only cars he'd seen on the trip so far. He didn't have to walk all the way up to see there were no survivors either. It was too gruesome to describe.

"Okay, we'll put in a care package for you then, but I need you to find a secure location for a big drop."

"Why?" King asked, suddenly suspicious and his back itched as if he could feel a target being painted on him.

"You're about to have company," Sandra said sweetly.

King had almost completed an about-face and was ready to jog when he realized her delivery and words didn't seem to match up.

"Come again?" Michael asked.

"John Norton and the gang. They are pushing north, trying to get ahead of the Caliphate's column. See if they can get some long guns to bear on their fearless leader."

"This area's thick with feds," King said.

"I know, and John knows the risks as well. The government won't resupply them, so we've rerouted some of our own stocks and captured materials to send to him. That's why, when you find a good spot for a drop, I need you to use the cipher we agreed on."

"Roger," Michael said.

King could hear the twin diesels firing up before he saw the big vehicle moving his direction slowly.

"What general area are you looking at?" Michael asked over the radio.

"Head toward Lincoln Nebraska, we'll sort out the details later," Sandra said.

"Sounds good. How's my little buddy doing?" King asked, his voice sounding like two boulders rubbing together.

"Chris is mostly good. He's a challenge sometimes. With Blake gone so much, it's harder than I thought it would be."

"He'll be back soon," King told her. "And the body snatcher?"

King was the one who'd given the baby that nickname; not until it was born or they had a proper ultrasound could they start looking at names, let alone nicknames. Calling it 'The Baby' was too impersonal and, besides, Chris loved the nickname.

"Getting impatient to get out. By the feel of it, he's going to be competing in karate tournaments soon. Speaking of which, he's kicking my bladder. You two stay safe. Sandra out."

"Take care of yourself," he said and pulled the earwig out while Michael and his mother talked.

It had been a while, and he knew that the young man needed to reassure his momma that he was healthy, happy, and fine. Following the somewhat recent death of her husband and Michael's father, they were both healing by throwing themselves into their work. Whether the history books would remember this as a revolution, a civil war, or an invasion wasn't for King to decide, but he knew however it would be, that the actions of Michael, his mother, the Jacksons and people like John would be recorded for the world to see and know. He knew it wasn't in the cards for him, and he didn't want it. He liked the non-notoriety.

5

KHALID

"Sir, our rear column coming out of Texas was ambushed, and we have reports of militia groups taking pot shots at us up and down the country," Hassan, an American-born Muslim and radicalized Jihadi told the leader of the New Caliphate.

He'd been a veteran, retired. He'd taken to the DHS after 9/11 because he felt it was his 'Patriotic Duty', but knew that it was easier to slide into a position at a low level and work his way up slowly, feeling out his coworkers and seeing if any others felt as he did. He wasn't surprised at how many did and secretly wanted to transform the USA.

"Are we suffering massive losses?" Khalid asked.

"No sir, just a dozen or so trucks in Texas. Very few causalities anywhere else."

"Good. I want every airport within one hundred miles of our advance shelled and rendered unusable. Has that been happening?"

Khalid's time in America, though short, had blunted his accent some. It was still noticeable, but he'd been spending a lot of time with his cousin Hassan since they'd had a chance to catch up face to face.

"Yes, it has. I've also got another report here. Scouts in Nebraska had made contact with the local agents and were shelled by a Russian APC or tank. The men making the transmission were able to get away, but said that they were being fired upon from over the horizon."

"Do you think it's our Texas friend John Norton?" Khalid asked.

"I'm unsure. We've got two of their scrambled channels cracked and radio intercepts today show that if he isn't in Nebraska already, he soon will be, with a group."

"A group," Khalid said with a rare smile. "We'll crush the infidels, no matter the size of the group, the militias *or* the armies. We will wipe the slate clean here in America and end thousands of years of Christian bigotry and hate. If we could, Israel would be gone too."

"I thought our North Korean friends were working on that?" Hassan asked with a raised eyebrow.

"They are. Next to the Russians, they have the most capable military left in the world."

"And the Chinese?" Hassan asked, surprised.

Khalid just smiled at his cousin.

"Since the American President is no fan of John Norton's, perhaps we should let these scum thin each other out. Can you get word to the DHS that this Norton will be in the area? If they cannot get the job done, we will be there soon enough, in force."

"Of course. Allah Akbar!" Hassan was already starting to move and back out of the command tent.

"Allah Akbar," Khalid said stiffly, watching his cousin leave.

"Soon, it will be too cold for tents," Khalid said to the empty room, glowing from two computer sets and the blinking lights of radio equipment. "But we'll overwinter someplace nice. Florida perhaps? Georgia?"

Nobody was listening, and nobody answered.

6

JOHN NORTON, ARKANSAS

"We done for the night?" Stu asked John.

"Yeah, we go any faster and we're going to start losing vehicles. Besides, it's a good point to stop and refuel," he said smiling and pointing at a chrome fuel tanker truck that had died on the side of the road.

"Bet you it's already been drained."

"We betting on desserts?" John asked, holding a hand out to shake on the deal.

"Yeah, sure. I always get the nut loaf."

Caitlin snickered at that. The cake or brownies they got in the MREs were horrible, but about a thousand times better than the food itself. To bet for desserts was a favorite pastime for people who had little else to bet with. Things they could give up and not die because of it, that is. Still, the wording made more than couple of them grin.

"Got it," Tex said, sliding out of the back door of the crew cab and walking over.

He pulled out his knife and jumped up on the rear step. He held onto the ladder with one hand and tapped with the knife. It rang out hollowly. Stu start to grin at John smugly when John motioned to Tex to get on with it. At the halfway mark, the hollow sound changed. John shot back a smile, and Stu tried to hold in a groan.

When he'd wanted to report to duty, he'd been assured that it would count, working with John. He hadn't had to travel far and, from the get-go, they had been in the thick of fighting... but he wasn't sure that, without normal supply drops, their living on foraged and scavenged food and materials would hold out long... Unless they wanted to switch over to AK47s. Some of the men and women already had, even though their M4s were superior weapons to the AK. The ammunition was easier to find lately; the Jihadis brought it in by the truckload, apparently.

"John, why don't we go after the source, where they are landing?" Stu asked forlornly, already missing his dessert.

John had thought of that himself, but the intel coming out of Mexico and Central and South America was slim to none.

"We don't have the resources to do that. The federal government is supposed to be working on a diplomatic solution. The cartels run a lot of that area, so I don't know how effective that will be."

"I heard the Navy was fighting on the East Coast, to keep the North Koreans away from our coastal cities," Caitlin said, "but it wouldn't surprise me if we recalled some of our fast attack subs to start shooting some of the Caliphate's boats out of the water."

"Who says they aren't already?" Tex asked.

"True," John said., "Now, let's get a quick camp setup after we refuel. I want to be ready to push on in the morning."

With the windows rolled down, the cool air kept them awake. None of the group stayed at camp long enough for breakfast. Instead, they ate cold rations as they drove northward. The fuel tanker had topped off everything they were driving, and every jerry can they held. It wasn't the first one they'd encountered on the road, nor would it be the last.

Stu drove the lead vehicle, an old Chevy one ton. its white paint flaking off to show the gray primer underneath. It had been outfitted with an old CB radio that had had the crystals changed to get more frequencies, as did all the vehicles in the small convoy. The highways were starting to get cleared, either by government workers, civilians or small townships, to make travel easier and faster. John mused that it was better now than it was two months ago, but coming through the major cities still had everyone on edge.

"Swing north now," John said, tracing their route on a fold up map.

Stu grunted and was about to make the turn to the exit ramp when the top of the truck was tapped by one of the men in the back who was tasked with being a lookout. Stu slowed down enough to be heard, and slid open the rear central window.

"Roadblock ahead, just past the curve of the ramp. If we take the exit, we'll be exposed on the sides."

"Who are they?" John asked as the column came to a halt behind them.

"Looks like townsfolk. No uniforms, ragtag weapons," the man said, leaning down to talk through the window easier.

"Want to do a sneak and peek with me?" John asked Stu who was already checking his vest.

"Oh yeah."

"They saw us coming," the lookout told them. "They

have half a dozen guys walking in this direction. I counted a dozen at first glance, but it's probably more like twenty. We parked in a low spot, so I lost sight of them."

"Okay. Go back and tell the rest of the column for me. No radios, these boys might have their ears on. Tell Caitlin to get the small mortar set up. If shooting starts, I want the roadblock and everyone staffed at it turned into a pink paste."

"Yes, sir," he snapped off a quick salute and then hurried off, the truck rocking as the men in the back climbed out.

Stu checked his handheld and put in his earwig. John did likewise, and once a quick check of their weapons was done, they walked along the side of the highway. This section had been cleared as well, but within thirty seconds they could see cars pushed into the middle, from the median to the far side of the road, where cars were lined up on either side.

"Want to bet they're going to ask for a toll?" Stu whispered as they took cover behind what was once a new Camaro.

"No bet," John said. "I got the luck going with me lately."

"Yeah, who scores two brownies in a row?" Stu grumbled as he broke cover and moved up.

Leapfrogging their movements and covering each other, they made their way forward a quarter of a mile in no time. The flat, downward sloping land gave visibility farther than they had expected, which meant they had probably been spotted a long while back themselves.

"Here we go," John said and then held up a finger.

Six men dressed in dirt-covered jeans and t-shirts and sweaters walked down the center of the highway. Of the six, five of them carried deer rifles of various makes and calibers, but the sixth had an old pump action Mossberg 12 gauge.

"Think there's any chance they have a doctor with them?"

"All we can do is ask," the man with the shotgun said, "unless it's those Caliphate jackholes."

"Frank said they were Anglos," another piped up.

"Anglos can be Muslim too, ya racist."

"I ain't no racist, I'm dating your momma, ain't I?"

"My momma? Why you lying sack of—"

"Hey guys, for real," Shotgun said, "We need to see if this group can help us. They're gonna think we're a bunch of dumb ass rednecks if we come up to them arguing and fighting."

"Too late," John said, rising slowly so his head was barely over the top of the car they were taking cover behind.

Below their sightline, John motioned for Stu to stay down, stay put. He nodded, even though John's focus was on the group. They startled, but didn't go for their guns.

"Holy... Mister, you just about scared the life out of me," Shotgun said.

"Wow, you with that group that's coming up the roadway?" One of the men asked, a lever action gun slung across his back.

"Yeah, forward scout. Coming to see why you've got the road blocked and what your intentions are."

"Shoot, we're not really blocking the road, more like making sure our town doesn't get a ton of unwanted visitors. We're letting just about everything through as long as they don't take the exit through our town."

"Why you keeping people out of your town?" John asked, and motioned for Stu to circle around and come up.

"Last time we had a group come through, they fouled up

our water. Adults and kids got sick. Another one used it as a chance to scout us out, and we were attacked a day later."

"How do you know they were scouting you?" Stu said standing up.

"Holy JEEBUS!" Shotgun cried, holding a hand over his heart, his chest heaving. "You guys don't have to do that."

"Sorry," Stu said with a grin. "How did you know, though?"

"Because we killed one of the attackers," one of the six said, this one carrying a bolt action, "and it ended up being one of the folks who came through a few days before. Lately, we've been worried about that Caliphate, and we're hearing a lot about a big roving band of cannibals. They file their teeth, ya know."

"File their teeth?" John asked, an eyebrow raised.

"Yeah, to points. Like those old rock and rollers in the late 70s," answered a man who hadn't spoken before.

"You hear about that, Stu?" John asked.

"No, but I can ask the others. I'm Stu, this is John, we're... militia. We overheard you saying you were looking to see if we had a doctor; how come?"

They all introduced themselves and Shotgun, who turned out to be a Steve, answered. "Some of those who got sick with the bad water aren't getting much better. Dehydrated, got the sick coming out both ends. We're asking not forcing, to be clear, we can pay for services."

That alone put both men at ease. John turned his radio to the tactical frequency his team used and hit the PTT. "Caitlin, pack up and get the column up here. I need two medics in the front to deal with potential dysentery cases in the local town. So far, everyone is friendly."

"Got it," Caitlin said back into his ear, and he nodded, pulling the earwig out.

"What would've happened if we weren't friendly?" Shotgun asked.

"We had an 80mm mortar set up. The roadblock would have been cleared, and all people would have been vaporized," Stu answered for John.

"Who are you guys, really? No militia has mortars, not the ones we hear about on the radio."

"Irregulars," John said, walking up and holding out his hand.

"We rolling into town, setting up a perimeter watch while we're there?" Stu asked.

"Yeah, same as we did for the holding action in Abilene."

"Abilene? Texas? That was you folks?" Steve asked.

"Yeah, what of it?"

"You're the boys and girls who are kicking the Caliphate in the nuts every chance you get, aren't you?"

"Something like that," John said with a grin. "Now, let's go see what we can do to help."

7

BLAKE & SANDRA, THE HOMESTEAD, KENTUCKY

It would be a weekend of rest and relaxation when Blake finally sat down with his entire family. He'd gone to Massachusetts as promised and made his recommendations. He had almost called for Silverman to go with him, but in the end, he didn't. Tehn he'd regretted it as the governor and the local FEMA director had been almost as bad as what he'd had in Kentucky. He'd offered his opinion as such, and had also told the governor that his head had become swollen with power.

Not that he expected the president to act on his recommendations, but he'd seen that the tough coastal people were chafing under the strict rules and curfews enacted by the government. Not everyone there wanted to work in the camps, building transformers or winding copper to rebuild components. Some wanted to take their fishing boats out, or even get them back. A lot of the boats had been first docked to prevent misunderstandings as the naval warfare heated up on the east coast in the early part when the New Caliphate was trying to launch their land campaign. Now, they sat at the docks under guard by order of the governor.

The reason? Without the boats and a way to fish for themselves and others, they would have to remain working at the camps to get their rations. Forced dependence. Blake told the governor of Mass. what had happened to Boss Hogg and the ultimate shelling, and suggested that if he didn't change his style and ways that he might find himself in the same sort of situation before too long. It boggled Blake's mind that a higher densely populated state had been brought under the man's thumb so easily. He made his suggestions to open the camps, allow the fishermen who wanted to fish to go back to work, and see if people outside of the cities would like to come in. It would do more for morale than anything else.

Production levels would rise, tempers would cool and, although everyone knew that the components needed to be built, building them with a gun to their figurative heads didn't exactly make products that met quality standards. Blake had been cussed out, threatened, and run out of town. He smiled at the memory of the governor's face going almost purple. He'd scored points with the regional FEMA director who saw a lot of merit in what Blake was saying, but he doubted he'd get enough hands to work on the component builds without compelling people to stay and work.

"What are you smiling about, sir?" the helo pilot asked through the headset.

"That whole thing back there," Blake said, pointing behind him.

They were on their second leg of the journey, with one more refueling left to get him to the Homestead.

"The governor? I heard about him. I thought you might have some fun," he said grinning, but facing forward.

"If the folks upstairs knew how I was going to react, they had to know what I'd suggest."

"Probably, still, maybe they are using you to gauge how bad things really were."

"Could be. I just don't understand why they don't get that you can't enslave people and then wonder why they are unhappy. That's the reason we fought off the British."

"Hey, you don't have to convince me. I hear this is going to be one of your last trips with us."

"It's my last," Blake said. "I got it in writing."

"Yeah, I was retired too, got mine in writing. Now look at me."

Blake thought about that and leaned back, letting the straps hold him tight as he nodded off.

"DADDY!" CHRIS SHOUTED RUNNING TO HIM AS SOON AS HE got off the chopper and it took back off.

Chris launched himself into the air and Blake caught him. His leg and shoulder both spasmed in pain from the healed gunshot wound, but he had been getting stronger, and it bothered him less and less. Today he was sore from the long ride across the country.

"Momma said she hopes you found her a horse," Chris whispered into his ear.

"What? A horse?" Blake knew they were gathering livestock, but if his wife wanted a horse, he had enough pasture and feed, so he'd get her a horse.

"Yeah, she says she's gonna eat it," Chris said and cracked up.

Blake put him down, laughing at the joke, and they walked toward the house. A lot of the training, guns, and hand-to-hand was still done on the Homestead, but he could see that more and more of it was being moved to Sgt.

Silverman's outpost, judging by the look of the emptying field near the barn. The barn had been once used in the underground railroad and had dorm style housing, and it was still used as such by the folks who had come to live there full time.

"Well, then, let's go see her. How's your grandpa and grandma doing?" Blake asked, seeing Duncan lumbering out of the barn and heading toward him, a smile lighting up the pastor's face.

"Pretty good. Grandma has been making Grandpa eat his vegetables, so he says he's wasting away to nothing. He's still big, though. Momma said she's stealing his belly."

Blake smiled. Sandra had gained at most twenty pounds so far in her pregnancy. She had been all baby when he'd left close to a week ago, and she was hungry all the time. He'd have to go hunting and do something about that, though there was plenty in the root cellar and even more stored in the barn and in the barracks. Fresh smoked bacon was what she had been asking for last time, and though they were starting to hunt out the immediate area, he knew he could find game.

"Well, your grandpa needed to lose a little anyway. Are you eating your veggies?" Blake asked and poked his adopted son in the ribs.

"Yes, Grandma and Mom are cooking them up all yummy like."

Yummy like, that usually meant battered and deep fried. One surprising thing about the new diet was that people were eating a lot of things that the former experts in the country would have called unhealthy. Red meats, fats rendered into lard to fry with, deep fried veggies, wild game, unlimited nuts, and berries. Blake remembered that some at the farm called it a paleo style diet, but it had been one he'd been eating for a long time. More out of being frugal, and living a life off the grid and blogging about it. Now that there was no blog, he had his informal radio show, one he'd been neglecting. Still, he'd requested and gotten some items on his trips through the country that he planned on using. One of them was a working iPod, loaded with music that he planned on using.

If there were digital rights to pay, he'd send the President the bill, because he knew he wasn't profiting on Rebel Radio one bit, and two, that the economy was effectively shot. There were rumblings of some kind of credit system, some grumblings about RFID chips, some talking about tattoos with serial codes. It was all bunk as far as Blake was concerned. Nobody was going to be willingly tagged... he hoped.

"Blake?!" Sandra yelled, breaking into a run.

He didn't wait; he left Chris to eat some dust till the boy caught up as he embraced his wife warmly.

"Lord, I've missed you," she said, her voice thick with emotion.

"You too," Blake told her, kissing her deeply until wolf whistles sounded from the edge of the barn.

More than one rebel yell broke the rest of the silence that wasn't filled with the whistles and catcalls from the students but Blake didn't care. He was caught up in the moment and overcome with love for his wife, his family, and his life.

"Wow," Sandra said, breaking the kiss before it became R-rated. "What got into you?"

"I've missed you," he said hoarsely.

"I missed you too. How long do I have you for this time?"

"Till death do us part," Blake said and gave her a squeeze again.

"Easy, Dad, you'll pop the baby out early," Chris said, pushing himself between the grownups.

Duncan's booming laugh caught them off guard, and they turned to see him and Lisa walking to them hand in hand.

"Do you mean it? You're done?" Sandra asked.

"I even have it in writing. A dozen states in over a dozen weeks. The rest of them can follow suit or shut up."

"I heard about what you had to say to the governor. Was he upset when you saw him?"

"Which one? Ours or the one in Massachusetts?"

"Ours," Sandra said, dimples forming at the edges of her smile.

"I think Silverman was about ready to have kittens when I said that, to be honest."

"I'm sure of that, but what did the governor say?" Sandra asked sweetly.

"He looked embarrassed. I really think he's worried that what happened last time would happen again if they forced our hand."

"What, you mean America's last celebrity getting locked up in the pokey for not listening to him?"

"Locked up in the Pokey?" Blake asked, grinning from ear to ear.

"It's an expression."

"He's just worried that we have enough support to roll with a full division with armor, mortars, and artillery, maybe even some air support," Duncan said coming to a stop a dozen steps beyond Sandra.

"Oh, that I don't doubt. We could totally do that," Sandra said grinning, "if our Commander in Chief would come out of his bunker once in a while, and really talk to the people... make a difference... then maybe more people might listen to him. As it is, a lot of folks are questioning his motivations."

"How so?" Blake asked, feeling out of the loop.

"Well, the rumors of the president being a Muslim or an ISIS sympathizer have been circulating for a while now," Sandra told him, "and over half of his appointments have been folks of the Muslim faith, not that there's anything wrong with that."

"Yeah, but Christians aren't strapping bombs to their chests and blowing themselves up in crowds," Sgt. Smith said, and walking up he held his hand out to Blake.

Blake broke his embrace from Sandra and shook hands with the guardsman who'd thrown in with their lot and had provided the first real fangs to what had amounted to a centrally located military unit in the country. They'd become fast friends, and he suspected Smith had more than a few female admirers, though he only entertained once in a blue moon and never the same lady twice.

"We don't know that, not right now," Blake said.

"You're still a little out of the loop," Smith said. "We're starting to get information coming in from across the world."

"Anything new, or any rumors dispelled?" Blake asked.

"Naw, the North Koreans are Satan, Israel nuked Iran in retaliation to them trying to nuke them, and the missile defense system we set up in Poland worked."

"That's all?" Blake asked, somewhat sarcastically.

"No, Santa Claus has determined that everyone from ISIS is on the naughty list this year and they aren't going to be getting anything," Lisa said.

"Now that isn't—" Duncan started to say.

"Hey, is Santa going to come this year?" Chris asked, "He didn't come last year. My other momma said we were too poor and didn't have a big enough chimney for Santa to fit down."

The smiles went to choked silence and Blake turned, picking up his son. "He's coming this year, buddy. I promise you that."

"How do you know?" Chris asked.

"Because I was working for the government and NORAD assured me he could fly over the country this year. We might be in a war, but he's got a special tracker on his sleigh that lets our Air Force know he's a friendly."

"Yeah," Sandra said, walking up and crushing Chris between her and Blake.

"I don't have a baby in me, but if you two don't stop, you're going to squish something other than a baby out of me," Chris cried.

"Ewwwwwwwwwww," Sandra said, backing off.

They laughed. Things were getting back to normal.

"WHAT DO YOU THINK OF THE NEW GROUP?" BLAKE ASKED Bobby.

"Pretty raw. I worry that they may not learn enough before they go out there to fight. Many of them know as much as I do, and I don't want to go out there and fight the Caliphate."

"Not wanting to fight isn't a bad thing," Blake said, "I hate it myself. I'm better off doing my own thing than fighting, I think."

"Blake, since I've met you, you haven't been doing your own thing. Heck, from what Duncan and Sandra told me about your blog and YouTube channel, you weren't ever really doing your own thing. You were a born teacher and innovator. A backyard inventor and scrapper."

"You trying to make me blush? You know I'm married right?"

Bobby bumped his brother-in-law's shoulder with his own as he laughed. They were walking towards the back of the property where the old grain silo was. Blake had a notion of using it for what it originally was intended for, instead of a lookout point like they had been. It still gave him shivers, remembering climbing the silo the day after the planes fell.

"What are you looking for back here?" Bobby asked.

"I just want to get a feel for the game, and how much the added people have scared things away. Your dad still doing the foraging classes with the kids?" Blake asked, already suspecting.

"Yeah, we've gleaned as many wild foods as we can put up. This winter might be a harsh one, but we won't go hungry. Maybe bored with the food choices, but we'll have enough."

"That's good— "

Blake saw a flash of brown and brought his .30/06 up in one fluid motion. A whitetail, at least a six-point was caught in the open as some does crashed through the underbrush. The rifle shot was loud, and the hasty snapshot was spot on. The buck kicked its legs out after the shot and, as Blake worked the bolt of his gun, the deer bounded into the thick stuff bordering the edge of the old hayfield.

"Blake honey, was that you shooting?" Sandra's voice asked sweetly from the handheld radio.

"Yes, it was."

"I know I said I wanted some fresh bacon, but what I'd

really like is some tenderloin. A nice, fat deer would do if you would be so kind."

"So you don't want tenderloin wrapped in salted, smoked bacon?" Blake asked.

"Well, I wouldn't send the plate back to the kitchen if that's how it showed up," she said, both of them hearing the near laughter in her voice.

"Well, I think we can do that, as long as there's some bacon in the salt box."

"Goodie!"

Sometimes, what he knew about his wife and how she acted were two different ideas that were hard to swallow. King, the massive black man who had trained her, said she had surpassed him in both ability and skills, which made her one of the top ten operators still alive in the world. She was also five feet nothing, a pixie-looking woman who wore her hair short and looked absolutely stunning. Somebody so petite and innocent and saying words like "goodie" just didn't fit the mold of one of the baddest operators in the world.

"It's all for you, babe," Blake said with a grin.

"And the body snatcher! Sandra out."

"Blake out."

"I hope you killed this one," Bobby said.

"He's down, I heard him thrashing. You want to gut this one?"

"It still makes me puke."

"Good, then you need more practice," Blake told him with a chuckle, enjoying his time on the property.

He'd both lost a good friend and brother in Weston, but he'd gained Bobby, Lisa, and doubly cemented himself within Duncan and Sandra's hearts. Life was great.

8

MICHAEL & KING, NEBRASKA

"What you gotta do is put the squeeze on 'em, boy," King said, nodding to Michael.

A man in a black uniform and a DHS patch sat between the two of them. A campfire was burning high in a small clearing between a wooded area and some corn near a power station. A dead to the world power station.

"You mean, get his... you know?" Michael asked, pulling a pair of channel locks out of the fire with a damp set of pot holders.

The metal glowed a dull red color and the dark skinned DHS agent seemed to almost pale enough to make Michael look like he'd been out of the sun for months, which he hadn't.

"You two are making a mistake. You can't do this to us. Martial law is in effect, and the president has given us permission to— "

"Commit treason?" Michael asked, opening and closing the pinchers close to the captured agent's face.

The heat coming off them was strong enough to make him close his eyes.

"Taking too long," King said, pulling a knife out and striding over to the agent.

Michael pulled the big pliers back so the man could watch King walk up. With his hands tied behind his back, King lifted him to his feet by the neck with one hand and brandished the knife. He slit the belt in two pieces and cut a long tear down the black BDUs the agent was wearing, exposing a yellow stained pair of boxer briefs that may or may not have been white in the last decade or so.

"You done now?" Michael said, "Or do you want me to cauterize it while he's standing?"

"Cauterize what?" The agent asked, the smug tone in his voice now gone.

"Your wing wang, boy," King told him. "I'm teaching the kid here how to 'Lorena Bobbitt' traitors and turncoats. Which one is you?!" King boomed, using his free hand to make air quotes.

The question was a trap, and everyone knew it, yet the agent knew the knife was close to his groin, and Michael had put the channel locks back near the fire with the pot holders to let them heat back up.

"Neither," he said after a minute, sweat running down his cheeks. "I'm just doing what I was ordered to do. I'm not even sure if we're answering to the government any more."

"Who gave you those orders?" Michael asked, knowing King was using a lot more words than he usually did and was getting cranky.

"And who do you think you're answering to, if not the federal government?" King added.

The man spilled his guts. He had no choice. He truly believed he was about to lose his own, or King would go through with the castration as promised. The DHS had been buying guns and ammunition for years, stockpiling supplies all around the country. Billions and billions of rounds of ammunition. The DHS was there to fight terrorism and help keep order within the country. When TSHTF, they were suddenly the only agency with a working command structure and were given very broad powers to enforce martial law. They could work as judge, jury, and executioner. They could round up citizens and force them into the work camps.

They could requisition supplies from citizens and yes, atrocities and the ugly side of human nature did rear its head from those who were supposed to protect it. It wasn't everybody, but after a while, government agents who used to be treated slightly better than clerks were now holding a shiny black gun, a badge, and a mandate. The power went to many of their heads. Food for sex? Supplies for information? Filling the work camps fast and getting bonus time off? The lists were endless.

After a while, the captured agent didn't even have the knife held to him, as he sat in the dirt next to Michael and recounted what he knew.

"So why is it you think your people went off the reservation?" King asked.

"A lot of this is a rumor, but we were told Hassan Nadir, head of the DHS, disappeared right before the EMP went off, along with half of the top DHS echelons. I don't know for sure if they knew it was coming or were forewarned, but most of them showed back up, but not Nadir. Nobody would talk about Hassan, nobody in the top levels."

"Did he die in the aftermath of the rioting and burning cities?" Michael asked, remembering what it had been like going through Anniston.

"No, because orders come down the pipeline sometimes. The don't always have his signature on the faxes."

"How do you clowns have faxes when we got hit with an EMP?" Michael asked.

"Because we were prepared for an EMP. We have entire football field worth of underground bunkers full of gear, ammo, electronics, vehicles."

"How do you know all of that?" King asked, getting close to him, knowing his presence was intimidating the agent.

"Because I worked in supply until this month. I had to take an outside rotation."

"And you thought it strangely okay to meet up with Muslim men from ISIS as equals?"

The agent was silent for a long moment. "I was following orders."

"I wonder... no, I don't care. Where is the closest supply base, bunker thingy?" Michael asked, standing up so both King and he were looming over the agent.

"No way. Telling you this much can get me killed. I give up that location, I'm a dead man."

"Oh, you're already a dead man," Michael said coldly, pulling one of the Gold Cups from his holster, "But there are worse things than death."

"Oh yeah?" The agent said, a sneer crossing his face, the first sign of defiance in a long while.

The bark of his gun and the suddenness of Michael's actions almost startled King. Instead, though, he watched as the agent rolled backward as the heavy .45 round made the ground in front of his crotch erupt. The agent came to on his side, where he rolled back to his legs, facing the two men, not wanting to show them his back.

"The big man there likes knives," Michael said, a maniacal look coming into his eyes. "Me? I like guns, and small targets are something I like to practice with," he said, raising the pistol deliberately and taking aim.

"That's cold," King said. "Shooting it off? I haven't seen you this angry since we jumped those ISIS cretins in Oklahoma."

Horror stories were told of what had happened in Oklahoma. Ninety five percent of it was fabricated, and, every time the story was told, it was embellished. The agent had heard the whispers of the resistance group, and how some crazy team in the south was blowing up and killing terrorists in small lots. Never a lot at a time, but one such story was that when the DHS rolled up, the terrorists were riddled with bullets. They could tell that most of them had been done before death because they had all bled. Ankles to thighs were shattered with gunfire, then the victims were put down with a bullet to the head.

Michael hadn't done it, but they had both heard about it and wondered who it was. As it was, the look of sheer horror on the agent's face let them know he had heard the stories too.

"You wouldn't. You guys took an oath," the agent said in a whisper, still a hint of defiance in his voice.

Michael adjusted his aim slightly and pulled the trigger. The agent howled and jerked his head side to side, trying to staunch the flow of blood from the missing chunk of earlobe and probably popped eardrum.

"I'm not in the military," Michael said.

"I was convicted of murder," King told him, pulling the knife back out.

"Do you have a map?"

"YOU LEAVING HIM?" KING ASKED, NODDING TO THE AGENT who was ziptied at the wrists and ankles.

"Yeah, I'm going to take his boots, though. If he can walk back to where we ambushed him, more power to him, but I want him to go slow. Give us a couple of days to get ahead of him."

"Good thinking. Why not kill him?" King asked, curious.

"I mean, we *can* I guess... but he's really kind of pathetic. I don't believe the "following orders" bit; they could have quit... but I don't know if he's truly evil."

"Didn't have no problem making him think you were, though."

"I know, thanks for the Oklahoma dig. That scared the crap out of him."

"Wonder if it's true?"

"Yeah, me too. So you don't think leaving him alive is a screw-up?"

"What you think?" King asked, his voice making it sound like 'whatcha tink?"

"I... this is a teaching moment, isn't it?" Michael asked suddenly, realizing why King was letting him take the lead on both the questioning and decision making.

"Yup," King said, flashing him a big smile.

"Well, I think now that we've talked to him, it's... if he was holding a gun and shooting at me, it wouldn't even be a question."

"And this man hasn't done nothing we know of that makes him need a noose or a firing squad?"

"Yeah, you know, that's it. He's the enemy, but now that he's been disarmed and owned... He's going to have hell to pay if he makes it back to the DHS."

"He talked," King said.

"So, as soon as he gets loose he's probably going to go find a hole, jump in and pull it in after him?"

"Think so," King told him. "Let's get while the getting's good."

Michael walked over, a large bowie in his hands. The prisoner begged and pleaded, but the young warrior sliced the shoelaces of the man's black boots and pulled them off. Then he sliced through the waistline and belt of the agent, taking the boots with him. The blubbering stopped as the agent realized the knife wasn't meant for his flesh and stared at Michael with red-rimmed, wet eyes.

"What now?" He asked quietly.

"When we're gone, find a sharp rock. Cut the zip ties off. Don't follow us. And a piece of advice? Don't follow orders you know to be wrong. Otherwise, the next time you run across someone like us, we'll stick you in a hole."

"I can't go back, they'll kill me."

"Make sure we never see you again," Michael said, standing and walking towards King and the APC.

He really was pathetic, Michael mused. If they could get some firsthand intel, something they could give to Sandra to pass up the line, maybe the USA citizens could get ahead of the curve for once. He just hoped John's group would hurry up and get here before all hell broke loose. Last communication had them two days out.

9

KHALID, NEBRASKA

Endless fields of corn. So much food standing, ready for harvest, that it hurt Khalid's eyes. There was so much starvation in the world, yet right here in the heart of the USA there was enough corn to feed two continents worth of people. Instead, the farmers were paid to grow certain crops, some of which were turned into a biofuel to use instead of oil.

Even though Khalid wasn't religious, that secret still hidden, he marveled at the raw beauty of the land. Only in his travels through Texas and the rest of the American Southwest did he feel somewhat at home. Now that they were slowly traveling north, their numbers swelling, he felt out of place.

"Cousin, Sir..." Khalid said, sliding into the Hummer that they had acquired a state back.

"Hassan, please; join me," Hassan said from the passenger seat. "Sit, refresh yourself. We're at a refueling point, but soon we'll be moving again."

"It's about Norton. He hasn't come up anywhere yet. They are going to start looking."

"You're worried he'll attack us here? Where our numbers are the greatest?"

"No, but he's the biggest threat at this point. Most of the US military forces are concentrated near coastal cities. Only groups like Norton's, and militia groups out of Kentucky have the chance to strike at us."

"This is why we've been disabling airports as we go north. I am sure some planes will get through, and long-range bombers can fly from anywhere, but without men to support them with intelligence, they have to rely on less-than-accurate information. Hence the reason we are striking air force assets in the center of the country."

Hassan hadn't been clear, but Khalid had suspected as much. He nodded. It made sense to him, and soon they would be coming into the areas that the crazy preppers and survivalists called the bunker states of America. The federal government owned vast tracts of land and NORAD was one of the more notable bunkers that the average person could think of. Without eyes and ears, they had to rely on coastal assets. Soon they would, and they would start harrying their columns of trucks, APCs and looted vehicles with gunships and helicopters, but they had planned for that as well.

Every truck had somebody trained to use a portable rocket launcher. The old Stingers had been almost thrown away by the USA in Afghanistan and Iraq, too costly to upkeep and maintain. But for people who were making guns out of sheet metal, the rockets and launchers were valuable, quickly hidden and maintained until needed. Until now.

"Praise be to Allah," Hassan told his cousin, "but why are our forces heading to Colorado, of all places?"

"There's a command bunker there. It is believed that the

American President is there. You have said you have access codes to nearly every complex in the country—"

"If we do that, they may very well nuke us," Hassan said quietly.

"It is like a game of chess, yes? You start your opening moves. You force your opponents to react to your plays. Soon, you can make your aggressions known, and start removing pieces off the game board. When the time comes, you force their king to move, to react, to hide or to lose. Maybe this will be a grand bluff. Maybe the president is not there after all. And maybe, they will 'nuke' us, as you say, though that is highly unlikely."

"Not literally," Hassan said, "but I can get you the codes to gain access. We may need to resupply in Nebraska. The trucks are going to need a couple days for repairs, and we need parts."

"Make it so. How long until we get there?" Khalid asked.

"Two days."

10

JOHN NORTON, ARKANSAS

The town was in better shape than most that the team had gone through. There were attempts by the people to have a somewhat normal life, albeit one without power and convenience stores, alcohol and whatever junk food they wanted. Still, they had pulled together when the lights went out, and a local church had become the meeting place for the citizens who'd survived this long.

"Without testing supplies," the medic was telling John, "we won't know for sure. We can pump these folks full of electrolytes, give them a broad spectrum antibiotic and make sure the water is treated. It's all we can do."

"Make it happen," John said.

"Stu," John yelled.

"Yeah?"

"Do you know how to make a big sand and charcoal filter?"

"Yeah, how big you want?" Stu asked.

"Big. Something's in the water here, and until we send a scouting team north, upriver, I want to make sure this water is filtered, boiled and bleached."

"I can get on making the charcoal. We here for a while?" Stu asked.

"Twenty four hours, tops. Then a day's worth of travel to meet up with King and Michael and get resupplied. I'm due to check in with them and the Homestead soon."

"Sure, can I snag some of the guys to help me?" Stu asked.

"Get some locals if you can. I'm going to have our folks start scouting and make sure we're not being double-crossed here. I'm not worried about these townsfolk too much. Nothing triggered my spidey senses yet... Also, we need support for our combat medics and medicine supplies. Some things are worth more than gold now. Worth killing for. You'll be safe finding supplies and building a filter."

Stu nodded.

The town was literally seven city-sized blocks. The center of the town had held the business district which, for the most part, was dark and the windows and doors boarded up to prevent looters. When the golden horde never emerged, the shopkeepers mostly kept things like that in case they were attacked, and to make their town less appealing to invaders, like what had already happened.

"Hi, I'm Pastor Brown," a holy man said walking up, one arm in a bandage.

"Hi, I'm Stu. I heard you are having some problems with the water?"

"Oh yes. Come sit a moment and I'll tell you, and you tell me what it is you need."

Sitting was the last thing Stu wanted, but he'd learned quickly that nothing was done in this town without Pastor Brown. He sat.

"We're better off than a lot of folks here, but our water supplies have been sullied by the godless."

"What did they do?"

"When they couldn't take us by force, they threw the dead into the river, used it as a latrine, and I suspect poured some chemicals in, too."

"Well, my boss wants me to build a big filter for your town to use. I could use some help getting materials and labor. He wants to roll out of here in twenty four hours, so to get it done..."

"You need the sweat of many to accomplish your goals. If you want to get any sleep."

"You got it," Stu said, smiling.

"First, what do you need?" The preacher asked. "With regards to materials."

Stu looked around the town and noticed a hardware store, a convenience store, a gas station, bakery, and movie theater. The theater looked a little out of place in such a small city, but he figured most of the population here had had to drive other places to work, there wouldn't have been much of a local economy. So maybe the theater was the local draw for folks. Still, he thought the plumbing section of the hardware store may have what he needed.

"Two large containers to hold water. Rather large ones if possible. Stackable would be great, in fact. Do you think the hardware store may have something like that?"

"If they don't, I know where to get some. One of our local residents passed away when her medication ran out. She kept rain barrels and those big plastic totes with a wire cage around them to catch water for her gardens."

"An IBC Tote?" Stu asked excitedly.

"Yes, I believe that's what it's called. She's only got the big one for storage, though. We've been using that water as it's not from the river, but it went so fast, and we have so little rain..."

Stu and the Pastor took a walk and found that the widow had everything he needed. The IBC would sit on the bottom of a storage tank, and a modified water barrel would sit on top, with the large IBC's lid screwed off to accept the filtered water. Right away, Stu asked about charcoal making and started to explain it, but the Pastor spread the word. Every cook fire was dug through, and all the black chunks pulled out. They would have to make about a yard of charcoal still, but the Pastor got a couple of men to get a pile of hardwood pallets burning and then they would cover them in the dirt to let them smolder and turn into charcoal.

The hardware store did have one portion that Stu needed, though. Sand. Big bags of mason sand. Suddenly he had more help than he knew what to do with, as the gaunt community came out to help. The IBC tote was dragged to the riverside, behind an old auto shop, and filled with river water. Half a gallon of bleach was dumped into it (overkill in Stu's opinion) and allowed to sit for thirty minutes. The water was let out, and everything on the tote was left open to dry. Finding some dry clean burlap had also been easy, as one of the shopkeepers of "You Sew what you Sew" had a lot of it.

While John had a patrol going upriver to look for contaminants, the medics worked with families hit hardest by diarrhea and vomiting, Stu and the pastor worked on the water filter project. Holes were drilled in the bottom of the rain barrel and metal straps from the plumbing department were screwed on for sides of the thick plastic drum near the top. The bottom of the straps was bolted to the cage of the IBC tote, making it almost impossible to tip off. The holes in the bottom of the tank lined up with the holes in the open tote lid, so the hardest part was done.

Three layers of burlap were cut in a circle and fitted at

the bottom of the barrel then the mason sand was poured in. Not 100% sure how much of what to use, Stu planned on using it all. Several hundred pounds of sand were placed in, and then the charcoal, once it was ground.

"It may come out a little cloudy at first," Stu told him, "But this is how we did it overseas. Our people had this down to a science, but I was only a bystander then. I'm winging this a little bit."

"You are doing what you can, which is more than most have," the pastor reassured him.

They ran out of materials and had to stop what they were doing until the charcoal that was being made was done. In the meantime, Stu walked around the small town while he waited. The land out here was rolling hills and, with everyone cooking over wood fires, he wasn't surprised to see a plume of smoke out in the distance. Curious, he made a note to check it out later or ask about it with the scouts when they came back.

"There you are," John said, striding towards Stu.

"Hey, just stretching my legs some. We're waiting on the last of the charcoal to be made so we can finish the filter."

"Perfect! Hey, listen, I couldn't get you on the radio. Everything ok?"

Stu looked down and turned the knob on his handset clipped to his side. No red light.

"Must have let the battery wear down or bumped it while building the filter."

"Ahh ok. Good deal. Listen, I'm getting a bad feeling here."

"The people of the town? They've been awesome so far." Stu said, suddenly curious, but feeling like the bottom was about to drop out.

"I've got some news on the radio and want to roll out soon, but our scout team has gone missing."

"Who'd you send?" Stu asked, curious and hoping it wasn't some of the new friends he'd just made. Just in case the worst had happened; it was cold, but it was a reality.

"Sylvia and Ron, that husband and wife couple who linked up with us last week, and Jared."

"Part of the Kentucky Mafia?" Stu asked, using the nickname they had for people who had gone through the training at the Homestead.

"Yeah. If they saw anything, they were to break and run for here. We haven't heard back from them."

"Which direction were they headed exactly?" Stu asked.

John looked north, then to the river and then back north again. "Probably about near where that fire is," he said, pointing to the smoke Stu had noticed earlier.

"The pastor and his people can finish the charcoal and filter if you need me," Stu said.

"I have a feeling I do. You, me, Tex, Caitlin and some of the saltier hands are going to gear up and have a sneak. We'll leave the rest here to protect equipment and personnel in case we need them to pull our butts out of the fire."

"You're thinking the worst happened?" Stu asked.

John didn't say anything, just stared north. Stu clapped him on the shoulder and headed back towards the vehicle he'd ridden to town in. He'd stored his guns and non-essential gear when he'd started his construction project. Now it was time to get his kit on and put on his war paint. With any luck, they were just lost. John prayed they were only lost also, as he saw the sky darkening as the sun started to set. In all that excitement, Stu forgot to ask about the news John had gotten that had prompted him to come find him.

"Anything?" Stu asked.

"Nothing. Approaching a clearing where I think the fire is," John told everyone over the tactical radio.

He'd become the spear of the new scouting party, with Tex and Caitlin just behind. Stu was left to guard their six with several in between them for fire support. Everyone kept moving slowly, following the path John had made through the tall grass by the river. At many points the brush had gotten thick, but a natural clearing appeared as Stu caught up with everyone who was spreading out across the outer edges of the clearing. What he saw shocked him to his core.

Three figures had been crucified upside down as a fire burned between all of them. Dancing in a circle were mostly naked figures. At first, it didn't register with Stu, but it was almost an even mixture of men and women. Filth and dirt streaked their bodies, except where the rivers of sweat had washed the grime away. All were chanting and dancing except for one gaunt, skeletal figure. The figure was so thin that the loincloth it wore was the only thing preventing the group from identifying it as man or woman. A long blade was held loosely in one hand, and the chanting stopped.

Two of the figures on the crucifixes were flopping and moving their heads, the only part of them that was free. In a flash, the gaunt figure's blade flashed out, making the ground wet beneath their head.

"Oh hell no," Caitlin cursed, bringing her M4 up.

Stu walking into that sight and taking a glance, and the point when they all opened fire on the figures, felt like a lifetime to him, but in reality it was less than a couple of seconds. He recognized the face thrashing as his lifeblood ran out; it was one of the Kentucky Mafia. Stu sent lead inbound for the gaunt figure who spun as several bullets hit him.

The gunfire snapped the naked group's attention to, and they started towards the seven party rescue squad. They opened fire as men and women pushed and jumped over those slower than them. It was a horde. Still, none of them were armed with anything more lethal than chunks of firewood and a few knives. The seven of them had a full load out. In seconds, what had been a horde intent on overwhelming them, broke ranks and ran. Several tried to pull the gaunt figure to its feet as they went, but they were waved off. Motors fired up somewhere to the north of them and roared away as the night quieted down. Slowly, making sure they weren't being surrounded in the dark, they made their way to the crucifixes.

The air stank of cordite, blood, feces and body odor. Making sure every single body they put behind them was dead and not playing possum was a sight that would give them nightmares. Many of the dead had their teeth sharpened to points. Already, in the dark, the flies had found them. They bypassed the still struggling figure with the knife, after kicking the red streaked blade far out of its reach. He was stitched high in the chest and once in the side.

"They killed her," Ron sobbed, his voice weak.

"He's still alive!" Stu rushed forward.

He soon saw the crucifixes were crude structures, made from 6x6 posts. Blood ran down Ron's legs where his feet had been tacked to the post with what looked to be a section of rebar. His hands were similarly tacked to the crossbars.

"Oh sh... look at... Oh, Ron, don't look any more," Caitlin said.

Jared had finished his struggles and had expired during

the firefight. Sylvia similarly had her throat cut, but the naked figures had started to eviscerate her, her entrails left in the dirt. After half a glance, not all of them were accounted for. It looked as if a butcher had sliced sections off of the front and sides of one leg. John was the only one who didn't puke right off. Not knowing what else to do and feeling out of his depth, Stu motioned for one of the new guys to run over and help him. Supporting his shoulders, Stu worked the stake back and forth before pulling it from Ron's feet. Similarly, Tex pulled the ones holding his hands.

Ron flopped to the ground, lifeless. He'd passed out from the pain or horror almost as soon as they started to work on freeing him. A low chuckle erupted behind Stu, making him spin. Up close, Stu could see that it was an old man now, but hadn't been able to make that out before. Gleaming in the darkness was John's knife, and he was holding it over the man, who kept laughing.

"Why?" Caitlin asked him.

"Everyone... Every.. everyone has to partake of the sacrifice. It's all been foretold," he wheezed.

"Who are you people?" John asked.

"We are the Others," he said taking a deep breath. "We've always been here, waiting for the judgment of the wicked. Our time... our... it's now..." he coughed, having spent most of his energy talking, and he gasped for a moment before finishing, "our time is now."

JOHN WAS WIPING HIS KNIFE CLEAN IN THE GRASS WHEN STU walked up to him, looking pale. John was sickened by all of it, but had hidden it better than most. He would pay hell for it later on in his dreams, but this was something they had to either follow up on now or pass on. Considering his hard deadline to get to Nebraska, he had some impossible decisions to make. One of the problems was Ron, who was too busted up to be moved right away. In addition to the holes in his body from the crucifixion, he also had a broken ankle and several shattered ribs. By the communication John had gotten earlier from King and Michael through Sandra, they had to be there already.

Was there proof that elements of the government were co-opted by the terrorists? Or was the government working with or for them? It would be earth shattering news, and the two of them couldn't do much against a bunker that was hardened against nuclear strikes. Despite the security measures that were in place, there were also DHS and potentially NATO or Jihadis for all they knew. They needed intel. That's why they had the supply drop relocated one hundred thirty miles south of there, and that was still too close in John's opinion. Without knowing the base's radar capabilities and what they had stockpiled, it would be dangerous no matter what.

"WE CAN'T JUST LEAVE HIM, POOR DEAR," CAITLIN complained about Ron.

"He won't be alone. The pastor here is putting him up himself, and Sandra's got a militia convoy coming through here in a few days. Between what our medics gave him and what they are bringing, Ron will be in good hands."

"But his wife... He watched her— "

"Listen, we all know what happened," John's words were sharp. "Saying it out loud only makes it more real, and we need to keep our focus here. The other thing I was going to tell you all, is that Michael, King and I have been in touch, as well as with the Homestead. We're getting reinforcements. Our first mission is to recon the base and see. It's not one of the strategic assets bases, but somewhere the DHS has been stockpiling stuff. Early HUMINT says it is part of an old missile silo that has been modernized and retrofitted.

"What we *don't* know yet is whether Sandra's contacts within the federal government are going to even listen to this, or if they are complicit in it. Part of the supply drop is going to be some high-end digital cameras that we are going to use for proof. They came back with Blake when he retired."

"That hillbilly retired?" Tex asked, the irony not lost on everyone.

"Yeah, he's now officially retarded," John said, using vernacular more familiar to him, "and I heard that he had another colorful disagreement with the government officials."

"What'd he do, threaten to rain artillery down on them again?" Stu asked, having become a fan of the Rebel Radio broadcasts and a fan of Blake's in general.

Even when Blake was away, an enterprising kid on the west coast with a working iPod had taped earlier transmissions, and coordinated with Sandra to play old episodes from time to time.

John just looked at Stu with a straight face and nodded. Stu's laughter stopped in a choke.

"What?" Caitlin asked.

"That kid out in California has been replaying the transmission between Blake and the new governor. Seems he told Blake he could compel him to remain in service, and Blake reminded him what happened to the last governor and quoted some Jefferson to him."

"That kid has some cajones the size of Texas..." Tex said.

"Or he's just as tired and fed up as a lot of people are, and just wanted to be left alone," Caitlin said.

"Plus, Sandra's gotta be getting close to popping, isn't she?"

"February or March," John said, already looking at the maps again. "So she's got a little bit, still."

"Oh... well, when do we roll out? Are we still waiting till dawn?" Stu asked.

"No, we're basically ready now. I'm just trying to figure out where those cannibals could have gone. We don't have any intel at all about the 'Others', and I'm trying to get as much info as I can for the militia group coming in the next day or two. They are going to hunt these monsters down. We don't have that option. Unfortunately."

Everyone could see John was upset, and his focus was absolute. They made ready and, before the twenty four hour mark John had promised, they rolled before the rising sun.

11

BLAKE, THE HOMESTEAD, KENTUCKY

"Blake, you have to hear this," Patty said as Blake strolled through his living room, which had been turned into the main communications hub for the Homestead.

"What is it?" Blake asked.

"We just heard from King through the relay channel. They've got eyes on DHS and Jihadis meeting up and attacking Michael and him as a single force."

Blake swore, one of his most infrequent phrases, so vile that it made Patty giggle.

"Does my wife know?" Blake asked.

Patty turned a dial and hit a button, and Sandra's voice came through the radio, loud and clear.

"...I say again, DHS and Islamic forces are banding together in Nebraska. Their target is unknown. We've long suspected an inside connection. Your orders? Over."

"Wait one, over," a stern voice said in response.

"Mrs. Jackson," a smooth, cultured voice, free from all stress, came across the airwaves, on a scrambled military channel. "Can you provide me proof of your reports?"

"General," the stern voice said before she could respond, "Our intel on her so-called source says he's a convicted criminal and murderer. I was going to tell her to— "

"I don't know who you are personally," the general said, "But it would do your well-being, your career, *and* your health, a great deal of good never to interrupt me again. Over."

"General," Sandra said, recognizing the voice of the once Louisiana Governor and former Joint Chief of Staff's voice, "do you remember me and trust me? Over."

"I do, child, over," the general said, his voice making him sound like he could be twenty or ninety; it was silky smooth.

"My source was my war daddy. My mentor. If what he did makes what he saw invalid, take me out of the loop, sir. I'd go to war on his say-so. The same way I would on yours. Over."

The general's chuckle came over the scrambled channel. "I am ordering the DHS to cease and desist all operations for seventy two hours, other than humanitarian efforts. If you can get me proof, solid proof... it would go a long way toward— "

"General, this is insane, I – "

"You, sir, are relieved of duty," the silky voice said, "on my authority. You will be court martialed and brought before me for sentencing when you are found guilty. Unless you want me to have your base commander shoot you on the spot?"

"No, sir. Over," a chastised voice said.

Blake looked around the room, his eyes the size of saucers. Chris wandered over and hugged his adoptive father's waist. Blake hugged back and boosted him up.

"I understand there are elements that my counterparts

will not re-supply because of political differences? Over," the general asked.

"Yes sir, over," Sandra said in a small voice.

"I am going to have some hardware sent your way. You have been in charge of the national militias and organizing the non-military resistance fighting our land-based wars here in the States. What do you need? Over."

Blake's mind was blown, and he almost choked in surprise as he waited for his wife's response. Where was Sandra? In the barn? The backup radio set up in the barracks? After what felt like hours, but was probably more like twenty seconds, Sandra started to rattle off a list of supplies. The general stopped her once to get a recording started, and she started over, adding more than she had before.

"... and that's just a start, sir. What I need more than anything else is cooperation. At every turn, what the DHS and the UN/NATO troops are doing is hampering our efforts. Yes, the people are hungry, sick and need aid, but if we're going to fight this war, we need our own supply chain. Over."

"Are you sure of this, Mrs. Jackson? Over?"

"What do you mean, sir? Over?"

There was a long pause, "One woman. One woman who has over a hundred thousand volunteering souls waiting on her every word. Filled with patriotism, filled with the hatred of the enemy. Wanting a target. I can give you the keys to the gun lockers. Of the ten to twelve million souls left in America, do you want this responsibility? Over?"

"Sir?" Sandra asked, her voice cracking.

The front door opened, and Sandra walked in with one of the large handsets that piggybacked off the big antenna that was now set up.

"You and your husband are the voice of the American Militias. You are literally directing as large a force as the American Military, or what's left of it. You and your husband have become cult heroes of the apocalypse. I asked what you needed, and you gave me a wish list for one op. What do you need, girl? Do you realize how much is hanging in the balance? Over."

Sandra walked over to Blake, her eyes tearing up. She shook her head when Blake's expression was ready to ask her a question. She leaned into him till he took the hint and wrapped his arms around her. Patty and David turned down the volume some, otherwise, they'd hear duplicate.

"Sir, if you can make the DHS cease all operations for seventy two hours, I have units from Texas to Colorado with eyes on. Let me get you the proof needed and perhaps we can make a decision then. Over."

"You didn't say no; you didn't refuse when I told you the reality of the situation. You're just as I remembered you. Give my thanks to your husband, for putting up with such a strong-willed woman. I'll be in touch in three hours. Over."

"He can't be right," Sandra said.

She was working herself up, and Blake had sent Chris with his grandparents while he tried to talk his wife down.

"Why sure he is," Blake said.

"I am not in charge of..." her chest hitched and, although they were sitting on the bed, Blake lifted her onto his lap and wrapped his arms around her.

She leaned back into his tall, lean frame and, when the tears came, he held her tightly, running his hands through her hair to calm her. When she started to calm down, Blake spoke up.

"You know you are, hun," he said and let out a breath he hadn't realized he'd been holding. "It's just now official. I think the reason you and I didn't get black sacks over our heads and a firing squad was because of how well known we got to be."

"There's probably more to it than that," Sandra said, "but yeah. Your idea for a radio show to help people survive has helped others out... and it's probably saved our butts too."

"Listen, in a few months after the baby is here, you can really worry about things. Until then, do what you're doing now. Nothing has really changed."

"But I'm in charge of a modern-day *Red Dawn* scenario. I am not a Wolverine," she said with a sniff.

"Yeah, I know, but you've been training and organizing things for a lot of people. It's second nature to you. Just do what you've been doing. It's working. It may not work all at once, but it's working."

"How can you say that?" Sandra asked, pushing back and turning to face Blake. "They've moved halfway through the country already."

"Do we have a large army that can mobilize at a moment's notice, with mortars and artillery backup?" Blake asked her.

"No, not really, other than Silverman and Smith's— "

"So, what do you need, girl?" Blake said, making a bad imitation of the silky, smooth voice.

Sandra half sobbed, half laughed, then hiccupped and punched Blake in the shoulder before leaning back into his arms. He easily held her until she calmed again.

"Who was the general?" Blake asked.

"He's the guy who made sure I wasn't court martialed and got me sheep dipped. New documents. He was a member of Dad's church before he got into politics."

Blake snorted, "Politics kept him from the church?"

"Politics and the church? Like a vampire bathing in holy water. Too many sacrifices. That's why I stayed a ground pounder."

"You're my wife, and you've always been much more than you think," Blake said and kissed the side of her head.

"You're just trying to butter me up."

"Maybe," Blake said and kissed her for real, "But it's still true."

"Blake, there's something else."

"What's that?" He asked, feeling his wife's mood shift as her body tensed up.

"John's group ran into a pack of the 'Others'."

"I thought that was just a Midwest thing?" Blake asked, horrified.

His own dealings with a cannibal had nearly cost him his life, and had literally cost Weston's life, a man he would have been proud to have been a brother to.

"Some of his group were scouting and were snagged. John and a small team were able to save one of them, but he had been crucified, and they had ritualistically murdered his wife and had started to feed in front of him."

Blake said nothing, feeling his skin break out into goose flesh. After a long pause, he held her tighter.

"Are the rumors true then? Has this group been here all along? Before the nukes?"

"I think so," Sandra said softly, rubbing her swollen stomach.

Blake let her go, and she sensed he wanted to move, so she scooted off his lap. He headed out of the bedroom and came back a few minutes later with a couple of well-worn paperbacks. He had read them, but he hadn't mentioned them until now. The similarities between fiction and real life were too much to ignore.

"What's that?" Sandra asked, wiping her eyes.

"Of the fiction I keep handy, I've got the entire 'Ashes' series by William Johnstone. He had cannibal groups in his post-apocalyptic series. I'm not saying it's the same, but maybe you should read some of this stuff and see how much of it matches your reports?"

"What, the running around mostly naked, using old school buses to travel through the countryside wiping out people, and eating them? Or maybe it's the filed teeth and how they all need a serious bath?"

"From what I can remember of Johnstone's stories, they wore cloaks and stayed in cities. The rest of it seems to fit. At least what you've allowed me to hear." Blake sat back down next to her.

"I haven't kept anything from you," Sandra said. "I just know you still have bad dreams about the night you were hurt and Weston died... I just tried not to..." her words trailed off as she worked on finding the right way to say it.

"Make a big deal out of it?" Blake asked, and his wife nodded, turned and then crawled back onto his lap where he promptly put his arms around her.

"We have to come up a plan for dealing with them too," Sandra whispered.

"We will."

12

MICHAEL & KING, DHS STORAGE BUNKER, NEBRASKA

"Eyes on target," King reminded Michael.

"I've almost got their timing down," Michael told King.

King grunted, and they kept looking. They'd made ghillie suits out of local materials and had been sitting in the same hide for almost twelve hours. Both were uncomfortable, hungry, and had to use the bathroom, but the only movements they allowed were the infrequent words, and jotting notes on a small notepad.

"We bug out in one hour to go to supply drop," King said quietly.

"Should we start working ourselves back now?" Michael asked, his voice almost too quiet to hear.

"After this truck goes through the guard post."

Michael craned his head as far as he could without making the suit rustle and move noticeably. A lone Land Rover truck, an old 70s model, was kicking up dust on the long dirt drive towards a gate that was manned by two men in a guard shack. The truck slowed and stopped as the guards pointed rifles and the driver and passenger both opened their doors. Through the binoculars, it was too far to pick out what they were saying if they could have lip read, but it was the man in the middle who exited out of the passenger door who garnered their attention the most.

"Recognize him?" King asked.

"Same head covering as the jerk who fired on us. Could it be the same guy?"

"Willing to bet that the DHS enforces wardrobe adherence. They have a Muslim with them, one who looks an awful lot like the cat daddy we saw earlier this week. If he had a scar on his left cheek..."

"He does, a big one, from his ear down to the edge of his mouth."

"That's him. Let's bug out."

"THIS IS MICHAEL. WE OBSERVED ONE OF THE LIEUTENANTS of the New Caliphate entering the DHS bunker. Over."

"Michael, Sandra here. Get to supply drop. I'll have high tech goodies for you and team Norton. We've been green lighted up the food chain. Get us proof I can send to POTUS. Drop area will have air support for twenty minutes to load up and bug out. Do you copy? Over."

"I copy. Over." Michael said, feeling woozy from such support.

They had been operating in the shadows for so long, it felt like they had been on a seesaw and been stuck on the high side. Now their end was coming down, and it made him uneasy.

"Failure in this mission is not an option. Over." Sandra said.

"You got this," Michael's mother's voice broke in from St. Louis. "I have faith in you, son."

"Thanks, Sandra, thanks Mom. Love ya. Over."

"Love you too, over," Sandra said with a chuckle.

"I meant my mom... I love my—"

"You better not be looking to steal my woman, over," Blake's voice broke in.

"I wasn't, sir, I mean, I was telling my momma..."

"They messin' with ya son," King said putting a big hand on his shoulder. "Deep breath."

"We will not fail. Mom, I love you, I'll see you soon. Blake, you have no worries from me. I think as long as I have tall, dark and ugly with me, I'll die single. Over."

"Tall, dark, and ugly? Boy, you want some more PT?" King thundered from his own handset.

The channel erupted with laughter with everybody holding down the PTT. Michael laughed along with them and saw King smiling as well.

"One more thing," Michael said, "I heard a DHS intercept. They're looking for John. The president has put the word out. I don't know who you were talking to Sandra, but at least part of the government is hunting for him still. Over."

"I'll let him know. He isn't in danger from us, or who I'm working with. Sandra, over and out."

Michael sighed and put his handset back on the charging station and turned to King.

"Tall, dark, and ugly?" King asked, smiling again,."When's the last time we practiced some hand to hand?"

"I thought we had to get to the drop zone," Michael asked with a gulp.

"We do, just playing. Besides, when this is all done, I

think you and me are going to hang up our gun belts and head back to Kentucky."

"Why's that?" Michael asked, confused.

King just waggled his eyebrows at Michael a bit until Michael laughed. "What's her name?" he asked, in between trying to catch his breath and trying to imagine who King had fallen for.

"It isn't one in particular. I just like me a strong woman. Good thing Blake's a good man, he's surrounded by some purty ladies."

Michael nodded. One thing that he had noticed at the Homestead and the training grounds was that the men were largely absent. The world, the free one in the USA, was now dominated by women and children. The men in a large majority had been killed off. There weren't enough numbers wise. The militias consisted mostly of men, though it was open to anyone who wanted to join.

"So you're going to go to Kentucky, and settle down with some yet to be chosen lady."

"Leaving my options open son," King said, firing up the twin diesels of the APC. "You got the gun."

"You got it," Michael said, getting ready for the wild ride that would take them to resupply.

"It'll be good to see John again," Michael shouted over the noise.

"Yeah," King shouted back. "Maybe he can talk me out of this crazy idea I've got cooking up here," King said, pointing one big finger at his head.

"What idea is that?" Michael asked double checking that the main gun was ready to fire if needed.

"We send somebody in. Dressed as DHS. To get the lay of the land. To open the gates of Mordor for us."

Michael grinned at the reference and nodded. He understood, and a guy of King's size was not meant for subtle sneaking in under people's noses. But Michael had done it before, at least on a much smaller scale. He had an idea of his own he was kicking around, and wasn't sure how viable it was. By the sound of what King had said, they were thinking along the same lines. Sort of.

"You up for it, kid?" King asked.

"Am I ready?" Michael asked, not sure himself.

"You're as ready as Sandra was on her first op."

"How'd she do?" Michael asked, walking to stand next to the big man.

"She's alive. Got the job done."

"So will I."

King nodded. They both remembered Sandra's words: failure wasn't an option. Michael knew somehow he wouldn't. Only time and the help of John's group would tell.

=-The End-=

To be notified of new releases, please sign up for my mailing list at: http://eepurl.com/bghQb1

ABOUT THE AUTHOR

Boyd Craven III was born and raised in Michigan, an avid outdoorsman who's always loved to read and write from a young age. When he isn't working outside on the farm, or chasing a household of kids, he's sitting in his Lazy Boy, typing away.

You can find the rest of Boyd's books on Amazon & Select Book Stores.

boydcraven.com
boyd3@live.com

Made in the USA
Middletown, DE
21 March 2019